FROGS SWALLOW WITH THEIR EYES

**BABOONS WAITED ON TABLES
IN ANCIENT EGYPT**

FLIES TASTE WITH THEIR FEET

**TORNADOES CAN MAKE IT
RAIN CRABS**

TORNADOES CAN MAKE IT RAIN CRABS!

WEIRD FACTS ABOUT THE WORLD'S WORST DISASTERS

A WEIRD-BUT-TRUE BOOK

**by
Melvin & Gilda Berger
illustrated by Robert Roper**

SCHOLASTIC INC.
New York Toronto London Auckland Sydney

ISBN 0-590-93995-5

12 11 10 9 8 7 6 5 4 3 2 1   7 8 9/9 0 1 2/0

Printed in the U.S.A.   40

First Scholastic printing, March 1997

WEIRD WEATHER

RAINING CRABS

In May 1881, a tornado touched down off the coast of England. The twisting winds sucked up hundreds of crabs from the water. The air currents carried them over the land. Finally the gusts slackened over the city of Worcester. And it rained crabs!

ANIMAL ANTICS

Crabs are not the only animals to be lifted into the air and dropped to Earth by tornadoes.

- Fish fell on Glamorgan, Wales, in October 1859.

- Snails fell on Padeborn, Germany, in August 1892.

- Worms fell on Halmstead, Sweden, in January 1924.

- Jellyfish fell on Frankston, Australia, in October 1935.

- Birds fell on Pageland, South Carolina, in May 1942.
- Frogs fell on Memphis, Tennessee, in October 1946.

> **DID YOU KNOW?**
>
> - Tornadoes are also called twisters or cylones. The powerful winds topple the biggest trees. The low air pressure blows buildings apart. And the strong updraft carries heavy objects.

LUCKY BLOW

The date was May 29, 1986. In China, twelve youngsters were on their way to school. Suddenly a tornado came swooping down. The roaring wind grabbed the students and carried them 12 miles! The gusts then dropped them on some big sand dunes. All were terrified. But no one was hurt. What some kids will do to miss a day of school!

TERRIBLE TIME

Tornadoes lifted four 100-ton industrial buildings in Monticello, Indiana, off their concrete pilings and plopped them down in a lake!

In April 1974, over 100 tornadoes hit the United States in just eight hours! The violent funnel winds blew hard all the way from Alabama to the Canadian border.

Brandenburg, Kentucky, was hit especially hard. Winds of up to 300 miles an hour destroyed nearly half the town's houses, stores, and factories!

The winds tossed a Xenia, Ohio, school bus onto the roof of the school!

A train passing through Ohio was carrying a shipment of new cars. The tornadoes broke the windows and dented the bodies of every single car!

LAUGH LINES

Joe: Was your house damaged by the tornado?

Moe: I don't know. I haven't found it yet!

PENNIES FROM HEAVEN

In June 1940, a tornado picked up a treasure chest in Gorky, Russia. The mighty whirlwind smashed the chest and scattered 1,000 silver coins over the city!

LAUGH LINES

Why did it rain money during the tornado?

Because there was a "change" in the weather!

WITH A SONG

A 1958 Kansas tornado swept a woman a distance of 60 feet. When she landed she found a surprise. Lying on the ground next to her was a recording of the song "Stormy Weather!"

DID YOU KNOW?

An average of 1,000 tornadoes a year strike the United States. Most occur in the Central Plains states.

FREAKY TORNADO FACTS

- An 1883 tornado stripped a tree in Illinois of all its bark—but the tree lived on!

- In St. Louis in 1896, a tornado drove a plank of wood through a half-inch steel plate!

- An Australian tornado passing over water in 1898 raised a spout nearly one mile high!

DID YOU KNOW?

- Tornado winds blow clockwise in the Southern Hemisphere. But they blow the opposite way in the Northern Hemisphere.

PLUCKED CHICKENS

In May 1950, a tornado stripped several chickens in Bedfordshire, England, of their feathers. The birds were found naked—but alive!

LAUGH LINES

What did one tornado say to another?

"Let's blow this town!"

NUTSY NEEDLES

Would you believe a shower of knitting needles? Well, dozens and dozens of needles fell on Harrodsburg, Kentucky, in March 1856! The downpour was easy to explain. Tornado winds had wrecked a needle factory and tossed the metal rods up into the sky.

LAUGH LINES

Why was the girl in Harrodsburg surprised when a needle fell on her head?

Nothing like that had ever entered her mind before!

SOUND SLEEPER

A September 1981 tornado near Ancona, Italy, passed over a carriage with a sleeping baby in it. The winds hoisted the carriage 50 feet into the air and set it down 328 feet away. And the baby didn't even wake up!

FOR THE RECORD

The tornado that charged through Missouri, Illinois, and Indiana on March 18, 1925, broke all records:

> **Longest path**—220 miles!
>
> **Greatest width**—one mile!
>
> **Biggest area of destruction**—164 square miles!
>
> **Longest lasting**—3½ hours!
>
> **Most killed**—792 people!

WATERTIGHT SHIP

The clipper ship *Ananuac* ran into a hurricane while sailing around the Cape of Good Hope in 1889. Strong winds and waves opened big cracks in the hull. The captain decided to abandon ship.

Then something amazing occurred. The ship stopped taking on water! The men sailed on and arrived safely in port. What saved them? Seaweed. It had plugged up all the leaks in the boat!

DID YOU KNOW?

- A hurricane is a storm with winds of at least 73 miles an hour. The winds swirl around a calm, clear area in the center of the storm called the eye.

TREASURE TROVE

In 1767 a hurricane sank five Spanish galleons in Pensacola Bay, Florida. The ships were carrying five million dollars in silver and gold. The money has never been found. Now you know where to look!

DID YOU KNOW?

Hurricanes over the North Pacific Ocean are called typhoons. And hurricanes in the Indian Ocean are known as cyclones.

LAUGH LINES

What is the difference between a hurricane and a lion who stepped on a nail?

The hurricane pours with rain. The lion roars with pain!

WORLD'S WORST WEATHER FORECAST

In 1964 the Director of the Weather Bureau in Formosa predicted Hurricane Gloria would bypass the island. Gloria struck the next day. The result? 239 people dead, 89 missing, and $17.5 million in property damage!

DID YOU KNOW?

- **The Australian weather forecaster Clement Wragge was the first to name hurricanes. He picked names of public figures he didn't like. Later forecasters used alphabetical lists of women's names. Today, hurricanes are named for men and women.**

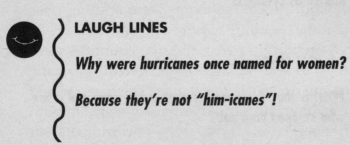

LAUGH LINES

Why were hurricanes once named for women?

Because they're not "him-icanes"!

A DISASTER THAT MADE A NEW COUNTRY

A horrible hurricane hit East Pakistan in November 1970. The winds battered the land at 150 miles an hour. That's nearly the speed of the fastest racing car! The waves towered up to 50 feet high. That's as high as a five-story building! Hundreds of thousands were killed or badly hurt.

The people blamed the government for not warning them of the storm. They complained that officials took too long to send help. The anger helped set off a revolt. Within a few months, the people had formed a new country. It is called Bangladesh.

A DISASTER THAT BROUGHT PEACE

Germany and the United States were arguing over control of the South Pacific's Samoan islands in 1899. In March of that year, the two countries were about to go to war. Just then a powerful hurricane came bearing down on the islands. The fierce winds and powerful waves sank many navy ships on both sides. Tempers cooled. The two governments sat down and signed a peace treaty!

WORST OF THE WORST

Most experts agree Hurricane Andrew, which hit Florida, Louisiana, and Texas on August 24, 1992, was the worst hurricane in United States history! The figures tell the story:

Homes destroyed—85,000

Homeless—300,000

Windspeed—164 miles per hour

Cost—$30 billion

Killed—33

Yet the numbers don't tell the whole story. There were:

Trucks blown on top of buildings.

Boats flung far up on land.

Mobile homes flattened like crushed soda cans.

Houses reduced to piles of lumber.

FAULTY FACT

People say "lightning never strikes the same place twice." Wrong! Lightning bolts often hit the same spot again and again. The Empire State Building is hit about 500 times a year. It received 12 bolts in just one 20-minute thunderstorm!

DID YOU KNOW?

- **Lightning rods protect buildings from damage by lightning. They conduct the electricity down to the ground through a wire.**

HUMAN LIGHTNING ROD

Ray Sullivan, a forest ranger in Virginia, had an odd talent. He attracted lightning—a record seven times! The first time he lost his big toenail. Twice his hair was set on fire. Other times he was burned on his forehead, shoulders, legs, and chest. The last bolt hit Sullivan while he was fishing—and he landed in the hospital!

?

DID YOU KNOW?

- **To avoid lightning: Stay indoors. Don't use a telephone or television. Avoid water. Crouch down if in an open area.**

NOT AGAIN

Workers finished the Petri Church in Berlin in 1726. But just as worshippers were about to enter for the first time, disaster struck. Lightning hit the building and started a fire! The flames were put out. But then lightning struck again. This time the church burned to the ground!

ST. PATRICK'S DAY SHOCKER

Mrs. G. Patterson was lounging in her bed in Baltimore. It was a stormy morning on St. Patrick's Day, 1990. All at once lightning struck. It exploded the bulb in a bedroom lamp. Mrs. Patterson dashed out and to her daughter's house. But things were no better there. Lightning had just hit her daughter's television set! Suddenly the telephone rang. It was her other daughter. Lightning had smashed her brick chimney!

THE LIGHT IN LIGHTNING

On July 31, 1947, a lightning bolt hit the University of Pittsburgh. The bolt carried 345,000 amperes of electricity. That's enough electricity to light 600,000 lightbulbs!

DOCTOR LIGHTNING

Edwin Robinson, age 53, was bald. He was also nearly blind and deaf after a bad auto accident. On June 14, 1980, a bolt of lightning hit poor Mr. Robinson. It knocked him cold for about 20 minutes. When he came to, he was a new man. He could see well again. He no longer needed his hearing aid. And two months later, his hair started to grow back!

HOW SHOCKING!

Right now nearly 2,000 storms are raging around the world. Every second they send about 100 bolts of lightning to Earth! Each bolt is a giant spark of electricity that jumps between a cloud and the ground. Each stroke carries up to 100 million volts! Compare that with the 110 volts of electricity in your house.

DID YOU KNOW?

• Flashes of lightning travel at about the speed of light—186,000 miles a second. Each bolt may be 100 miles long.

HAIRPIN KNOCKOUT

Minerva Bonham of Tory Hill, Ontario, Canada, will never forget the thunderstorm of August 1951. Lightning struck her head! But the damage was surprisingly light. All the bolt did was to knock out all her hairpins!

LAUGH LINES

Sam: I'm a conductor.

Pam: Orchestra conductor or train conductor?

Sam: Neither. I'm a lightning conductor!

OPEN SESAME

In 1952, lightning hit the home of Captain Bolling Williams of Biloxi, Mississippi. The bolt struck a

jewel box. It opened a latch that had been jammed shut for many years. What a lucky strike!

DOUBLE TROUBLE

A severe thunderstorm hit Marianna, Florida, in May 1951. The lightning set fire to two houses. One belonged to C. N. Horne on North Green Street and the other to S. H. Horne on South Green Street!

SIMMERING SUMMER

The summer of 1980 was very hot. The South and Midwest were hardest hit.

- Highways exploded, sending hunks of concrete flying.

- Thousands of chickens died of the heat.

- Crops were ruined.

- The 91° temperature and 85% humidity made Washington, D.C., feel like a sauna.

LAUGH LINES

Ma: How hot was the summer of 1980?

Pa: It was so hot that people took turns sitting in each other's shadow!

HOT TIME IN THE OLD TOWN

Chicago had a brutal heat wave in July 1995. The temperature boiled up over 106°! Officials delivered fans and blocks of ice to people who couldn't leave home. They set up air-conditioned buildings for people to cool off. Their efforts helped keep the death toll down to 500.

LAUGH LINES

Ma: How hot was Chicago in the summer of 1995?

Pa: It was so hot that your tongue got sunburned every time you spoke!

RED RAIN

It rained in Switzerland on October 14, 1755. Big deal! Except that this rain was the color of blood! The cause? Red sand from the Sahara Desert had blown over Europe. Drops formed around the grains—and fell as red raindrops!

DID YOU KNOW?

- **Rainwater contains Vitamin B12.**

LAUGH LINES

Tom: I hope the rain keeps up.

Dick: Why?

Tom: So it won't come down!

MUCK AND MUD

The village of Saint-Jean-Vianney is—or was—just north of Quebec, Canada. Heavy rain began to fall there on the evening of May 4, 1971. Quickly the soil turned soft and mushy. Roads became muddy rivers. People, cars, and even buildings got yanked down into the sludge.

Soon the rain stopped. The ground started to dry. But the town was not the same. Thirty-one villagers and 38 buildings had been swallowed up! The survivors packed up and moved away. Who could blame them?

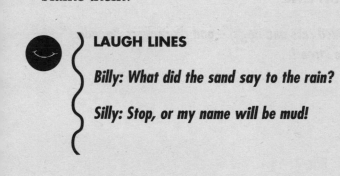

LAUGH LINES

Billy: What did the sand say to the rain?

Silly: Stop, or my name will be mud!

DROWNED TOWN

For 400 years almost no rain fell in Calama, Chile. The people prayed for rain. Finally, on February 10, 1972, a downpour flooded the town. The water damaged or destroyed every single building! It wiped out electricity and transportation. No one ever asked for rain again!

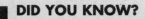

DID YOU KNOW?

- **If all the clouds were to change to rain, it would cover the entire Earth to a depth of one inch.**

LAUGH LINES

It rained cats and dogs—and there were "poodles" in the street!

SNOW TIME

A most bizarre blizzard pelted the western United States on January 2, 1949. The snow came down very fast. Within an hour cars, planes, and trains had stopped running. After three days the snow reached above the windows of most cars. Some drifts covered the telephone poles. Winds blew 80 miles an hour. Temperatures plunged to 50° below freezing!

Day after day the snow fell. Rescue planes dropped food and fuel to snowbound people huddled in their homes. Helicopters brought in doctors and medical supplies.

On February 19, the snow finally stopped falling. The blizzard had lasted a record seven weeks!

AGAINST THE ODDS

New York City gets nearly twice as many snowstorms on Fridays and Sundays as on other days. Of course, this makes school teachers very happy. It means fewer lost school days. But how do you think New York City kids feel about it?

LAUGH LINES

Mom: I've got good news and bad news. The good news is that school is closed today because of the snowstorm.

Tom: What's the bad news?

Mom: You have to shovel the driveway!

NOT WHITE AT ALL

Most everyone thinks that snow is white. But on January 31, 1925, gray snow fell in Japan. Scientists think it was colored gray by dust from an erupting volcano. The next year, on December 6, 1926, black snow fell in France. No one knows the cause. Any ideas?

SNOW JOKE

The New York City blizzard of 1888 caused much damage. But after it was over, people needed something to laugh about. One businessman put a sign on the pile of snow in front of his store: "This snow is absolutely free! Please take a sample!"

Another storekeeper used a different approach. His notice said, "Expensive diamond ring under snowdrift. Finders keepers! Start digging. You may be the lucky winner!"

FOR THE RECORD

Greatest one-year snowfall: 1,122 inches, February 1971 to February 1972, Mt. Rainier National Park, Washington.

Greatest one-day snowfall: 76 inches, April 14–15, 1921, Silver Lake, Colorado.

LAUGH LINES

A letter to the National Weather Service said, "My car just got stuck in ten inches of 'Partly Cloudy'!"

HAIL AND FAREWELL

The British king Edward III invaded France on October 28, 1359. His goal? To become king of France. By the spring of 1360, he reached France's capital city, Paris. Then, along came a freak storm! Large hailstones killed about 1,000 English soldiers and some 6,000 of their horses. King Edward III took this as a sign from heaven. He stopped fighting and made peace with his French enemies.

DID YOU KNOW?

- Hailstones form when tiny ice crystals blow up and down in a cloud. Moisture in the cloud freezes in layers, making the hailstones bigger and bigger. They grow until they are heavy enough to fall.

PUMPKIN-SIZE STONE

The biggest known hailstone fell in Coffeyville, Kansas, on September 3, 1970. It was 17½ inches around and weighed nearly two pounds! Imagine getting bopped on the head with that!

ICE MEN

In 1930, five German glider pilots accidentally flew into a hailstorm. They parachuted out of their planes. But the men did not fall gently to Earth. Instead, winds within the clouds blew them up and down. Moisture coated the men with layers of ice— and they fell to Earth as human hailstones!

ICE TURTLE

On May 11, 1894, a hailstone measuring six inches by eight inches fell near Vicksburg, Mississippi. Inside was a frozen turtle! Winds had probably lifted the turtle high into the clouds. Then ice covered it. Abracadabra. A turtle hailstone!

CATASTROPHES
BIG AND LITTLE

FATEFUL CRASH

The dinosaurs disappeared about 65 million years ago. At the same time a 200-mile-wide asteroid slammed into Earth. Scientists now believe the asteroid led to the extinction of the dinosaurs.

The collision raised a huge cloud of dust. It started giant wildfires that sent up thick, dark smoke. Erupting volcanoes added more dust and smoke to the air. The dark clouds covered Earth like a blanket.

Without sunlight, most plants died out. Without plants, the plant-eating dinosaurs starved to death. And without plant-eaters to prey on, the meat-eating dinosaurs perished, too.

 DID YOU KNOW?

- **The first dinosaurs evolved about 225 million years ago. They became extinct 160 million years later.**

KNOCK-OUT BLOW

A farmer was alone in his field in Siberia on the morning of June 30, 1908. Suddenly he was whacked unconscious. When he came to, he saw that trees everywhere had fallen, too. Why?

A 4,000-ton rock from space, a meteorite, had crashed down about 50 miles away! People throughout Europe felt the shock wave. Small wonder it bowled over the farmer!

DID YOU KNOW?

- Meteor Crater is a giant hole in Arizona. It is almost a mile wide and 600 feet deep. The hole was formed by a 100-foot-wide meteorite that slammed into the ground more than 50,000 years ago.

DUCK!

In November 1954, Mrs. E.H. Hodges was seated on her couch in Sylacauga, Alabama. Suddenly an eight-and-a-half-pound meteorite tore through the roof. The rock bounced off her radio and grazed her leg.

 DID YOU KNOW?

- **About ten meteorites strike Earth every day. But only seven people have ever been hit by meteorites.**

UP AND OVER

China's Yellow River has a history of floods dating back over 4,000 years. The worst came in 1887. The river washed over its 70-foot-high levees! The waters flooded thousands of acres of farmland. In some places the water was 50 feet deep!

TOWN ON FIRE

On the first day of June 1889, a dam burst above Johnstown, Pennsylvania. A five-story-high wall of water crashed down. It surged toward the city at about 60 miles an hour. The fast-flowing water swept up everything in its path. Soon the wreckage slammed into a big stone bridge! It formed a mass of trash and rubble that covered 30 square blocks and towered 70 feet high!

But the worst was yet to come. Hot coals mixed with some gasoline. The huge heap of debris burst into flame! The smelly, smoky fire burned all night and the whole next day. Finally there was nothing left to burn. The fire went out.

BAD NEWS–GOOD NEWS

Mrs. Lena McCovey lived near the Klamath River in Oregon. She lost a lot of her belongings when the river overflowed its banks in December 1964. Luckily her sister lived 200 miles downstream at Coos Bay, Oregon. That's where she found Mrs. McCovey's bottle of pills!

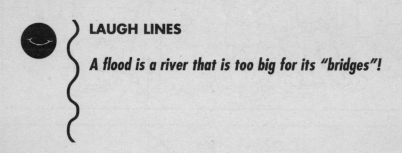

LAUGH LINES

A flood is a river that is too big for its "bridges"!

ICE MOUNTAIN

The *Titanic* made its first voyage from England to New York on April 11, 1912. It was the most advanced ship of its time. The 2,200 passengers on board felt very safe.

On the third day out, a sailor spotted an iceberg. But it was too late to avoid disaster. Within moments the ship struck. The iceberg cut a giant gash in the hull.

Crew members directed women and children to the lifeboats. But the *Titanic* was sinking fast. All at once there was a loud sucking noise—and the mighty ship disappeared into the black waters. Rescuers could save only 711 passengers on the "unsinkable" ship!

DID YOU KNOW?

- Nine-tenths of an iceberg is hidden under the water. The biggest known iceberg was about 200 miles long and 60 miles wide. That's bigger than the entire state of Vermont.

CAT'S TALE

One well-known survivor of the *Titanic* was the Englishman Gus Cohen. Since he seemed to have nine lives, his friends called him Gus the Cat!

After the sinking of the *Titanic*, Cohen served in World War I—but survived a severe head injury. During World War II, a bomb landed near him—but he escaped injury. Years later he fell out of a train and was hit by a car—but Gus the Cat lived to tell the tale!

BITE THE DUST

A long drought in the early 1930s changed the rich soil of the Great Plains of the United States to dry dust. The area became known as the Dust Bowl.

People and animals breathed the dust and got very sick. The fine dust clogged the engines of autos and other machines. Without water, cattle and crops died in the fields. Over three million farmers had to leave their farms.

At long last, the rains came. Help from the government arrived. Farmers learned how to save water. Workers planted trees to hold the soil. Other dust storms followed. But no more dust disasters!

DID YOU KNOW?

- **Most dust storms come in the spring. One reason is that the new crops are not yet able to hold down the soil.**

CRAZY CURES

Flu, short for influenza, is a virus-caused disease. It spreads easily from person to person. In the winter of 1918–1919 about 20 million people worldwide fell victim to the sickness!

In those days, doctors had few ways to fight the flu. So people invented their own often wacky ways. Many wore masks to keep from breathing the virus. Others rubbed bacon fat over themselves to keep healthy. Still others protected themselves by taking ice-cold baths!

DID YOU KNOW?

- **During the Middle Ages, attacking armies threw sick people over the walls of cities to infect their enemies.**

KILLER SMOG

The worst air pollution disaster struck London in 1952. Smoke from London's factories and thick, heavy fog made the air dark and smelly. This combination of smoke and fog is called smog.

The smog was so murky people could not see their hand in front of their face. Most everyone stayed inside. Only thieves felt safe in the streets. London suffered a terrible crime wave!

The smog blanketed the city for nearly three weeks. People could not breathe well in the poisoned air. Infants, the elderly, and the sick suffered the most. Many ended up in the hospital. Altogether, the disaster sickened some 8,000 people and killed about 4,000!

THE
VIOLENT EARTH

IN A TRICE

Martinique's Mount Pelée exploded at exactly 7:59 on the morning of May 8, 1902. Superhot steam, molten lava, and giant boulders shot out of the volcano. Three minutes later the blast was over. But not the devastation. The city of St. Pierre had only two survivors: a shoemaker lying on his bed and a prisoner in a stone-walled cell!

BIG BANG

Krakatoa is a small volcanic island in Indonesia. In August 1883 it erupted with a noise heard 3,000 miles away! The blast blew the island to bits! Even worse, it sent out giant 125-foot-high ocean waves, called tsunamis. The tsunamis wrecked hundreds of towns and villages along nearby coasts. Their effects were felt as far away as San Francisco and the English Channel!

DID YOU KNOW?

- There are so many volcanoes around the edges of the Pacific Ocean that they are called the Ring of Fire.

SURPRISE!

On the afternoon of August 24, in the year 79 A.D., Italy's Mount Vesuvius suddenly erupted. In a flash, tons of ash and lava buried the nearby city of Pompeii.

Centuries later scientists dug down through the lava. They uncovered Pompeii as it was at the moment the volcano erupted. They found a sentry still on guard, a priest at dinner, gladiators in the arena, two prisoners in their cell, and a barking dog tied to a post!

DID YOU KNOW?

- When the volcano Mount Etna erupts, it blows smoke rings into the air.

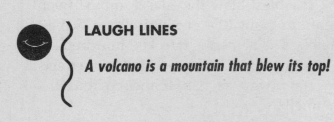

LAUGH LINES

A volcano is a mountain that blew its top!

MUD FLOW

Nearly four-mile-high Mount Cotopaxi in Peru erupted in 1877. The blow was small and little lava flowed. But something wild came later. The lava's heat melted the ice in the mountains. As the water raced down it became thick and muddy. The flow wiped out many villages—some as far as 150 miles away!

DID YOU KNOW?

- **Lava from an erupting volcano may be as hot as 2,200°. It can take years to cool down.**

ALL FALL DOWN

The famous San Francisco earthquake came early on the morning of April 18, 1906. The shock knocked over nearly 30,000 houses. But fire caused the worst damage. Flames from falling stoves and gaslights set the whole city ablaze. Broken water mains left no way to fight the fires. They raged for three days— and left 250,000 homeless!

DID YOU KNOW?

- San Francisco firefighters dynamited buildings to stop the advance of the flames. But often the dynamite actually started new fires.

A LITTLE LOOPY

Mount St. Helens is a volcano in the state of Washington. It blew on May 18, 1980. The disaster spread ash over hundreds of square miles. It also made the people a little loopy.

Some covered up the W on their license plates so they read "*ash*ington." When a baseball team canceled a game, reporters said they were "ashed out." A newspaper called the fourth day of the eruption "Ash Wednesday." And for those who wore handkerchiefs to keep out the dust, a bank sign read: "Please remove masks before entering the bank!"

LOST FARM

Dionisio Pulido owned a nine-acre farm just outside the Mexican village of Paricutin. Around 1940, he

noticed very warm soil in one spot. Deep rumbling sounds also came from this place.

In February 1943, the Earth began to shudder and the underground noises grew louder. Without warning, a column of dust, smoke, and gas hissed out of the hole. Small explosions tossed up ashes and red-hot stones. It was the birth of a volcano.

By the next morning a 30-foot-high mound of ash and rock had formed. Officials ordered Señor Pulido and the people of Paricutin to leave. More rock, ash, and lava flowed out of the volcano. Soon the pile was taller than the Empire State Building! It covered a circle of land about one mile across. Alas! Señor Pulido's farm was gone forever!

WORST U.S. EARTHQUAKE

America's most intense earthquake occurred December 16, 1811. The center was in New Madrid, Missouri. But chimneys fell in Cincinnati, 400 miles away. And people felt shockwaves in Boston, 1,100 miles away. The terrible quake even changed the course of the Mississippi River!

DID YOU KNOW?

- There are more than 50,000 earthquakes throughout the world every year. Of these, about 1,000 are strong enough to cause damage.

LAUGH LINES

The earthquake was so strong that it moved my house into another zip code!

TILT!

India suffered a terrible earthquake on June 12, 1897. The disaster destroyed every building in a 3,000-square-mile area! But one wacky thing happened. The disaster tilted the land upward. A quiet little river suddenly had a beautiful waterfall. And that waterfall still flows today!

WILD WAVE

An earthquake struck in the Pacific Ocean on March 3, 1933. The center was about 100 miles off the coast of Japan. The Richter scale, which measures the power of earthquakes, gave this one 8.9. The force equaled 7,000 nuclear bombs exploding at once!

The earthquake itself did not damage Japan. But the shocks set off a tsunami. As the tsunami raced across the ocean toward Japan, it sank about 8,000 ships. And when it smashed into the coast, it knocked over nearly 9,000 houses!

CAN YOU TOP THIS?

A giant tsunami slammed into the coast of Cape Lopatka, Siberia, in 1737. The cause was an earthquake in the ocean near Japan. The tsunami left its water mark on a cliff 210 feet above sea level! That's almost half the height of the Washington Monument.

EARTHQUAKE MONTH

Afraid of earthquakes? Then avoid Japan in the month of September. Earthquakes have struck Japan during September in the years 827, 859, 867, 1185, 1596, 1611, 1649, 1810, 1923, 1943, and 1965!

EARTHQUAKE YEAR

So far, the year 1976 proved to be the worst year for earthquakes. Major quakes shook Guatemala, Italy, Russia, Indonesia, China, the Philippines, and Turkey! The worst earthquake of all occurred in China on July 28, 1976. That quake killed 655,000 and hurt 779,000.

GIGANTIC SLIDE

On September 2, 1886, huge blocks of ice started slipping down from Rossberg Peak in Switzerland. The friction created such heat that the melting ice turned to steam and trees started burning. The sliding debris finally rammed into Goldan Valley and buried four villages!

GRAVE SAVE

A May 1970 earthquake in Peru started an avalanche. The snow slid down the mountainside killing about 18,000 people. A few did manage to survive. How did they do it? They hid behind tombstones in the graveyard!

SLIPPERY SLOPE

In January 1962, a two-mile-long mass of ice and rock loosened on Mount Huascaran in Peru. The fast-moving load sped down into the valley at nearly 250 miles an hour. It leveled the two villages in its path.

In the valley, the avalanche slowed to perhaps 60 miles per hour. The 40-foot-high wall of ice, rock, trees, and mud swept over everything. It rushed forward for ten more miles before stopping!

LAUGH LINES

How did the avalanche get to the village?

It turned left at the bottom of the mountain!

CHURCH BELLS

The loud church bells of Switzerland's Church of St. Nicolas started an avalanche in 1749. The slipping snow swept away the church. But it didn't harm the bell tower!

FIRE POWER

It was a frosty December morning in 1916. Austrian soldiers were practicing firing their cannons. Unexpectedly, the blasts set off an avalanche. Masses of loosened snow and earth slid down the mountain burying most of the men!

DID YOU KNOW?

- **Avalanches start when the snow gets too heavy. The weight causes a large block of ice and rock to break free and tumble down a mountain.**

DISASTER DAYS

The record for most disasters has to be southern Italy from November 1980 through February 1981. During those four months, there were:

- A major earthquake on November 23, 1980.

- A terrible blizzard on January 23, 1981.

- Another earthquake on February 23, 1981.